For Todd, Chase, Obie & Deuce
C.M.B

For Clint, Asher, & Cinnamon
A.F.

First edition 2020

This book was typeset in Loveland, Ohio.
The illustrations were done in pencil in Austin, Texas.

Pearls In Bloom Publications
Loveland, Ohio

MEET THE AUTHOR, WATCH VIDEOS & MORE AT

PearlsInBloom.com

Visit Celina's personal blog, ChasingChaser.com for more updates on
upcoming projects, devotions, and inspiration behind our products.

When I first met Obie, I knew **there was something very special about him.** He was sitting in a bed of bright green grass and there was a radiant glow that burst through the tiny white hairs that covered his tiny white face. He was only two-months old.

The day he arrived was magical indeed. I knew he would forever be my baby. He was the most pleasant gift from my love.

I would tease and say that he was my first hairy-born child.

I rocked him like a baby and even baked him birthday cakes—and soon our family expanded.

We now had another tiny white friend that we called Cousin Deuce.

(Actually, they really are real-life cousins. How is that possible you might ask? You see, their mothers are sisters and that's how.)

Together, they traveled in jet planes, crossed over mountain passes, and climbed boulders with not much effort at all.

Our family grew once more. This time our new little friend didn't have a face covered in white fur nor did he have little round brown eyes. Our new baby was human—just like you and me.

Life went on, memories were made. More birthday cakes and balloons were had.

I cannot be sure of the date, but one afternoon, Obie walked into the living room and made a grand announcement.

"I have decided to become a scientist!"

"Oh!" I replied. I mean what else could I say?

"Yes," explained Obie. "You see becoming a scientist seems to be the most logical career path."

"Career path? **But you're my little white dog and I love you that way.**"

"Yes," said Obie, "But little white dogs can't solve life problems or discover ways to grow food on Mars."

"Well, that's true I suppose, but I don't think..."

"It's settled," Obie interrupted. "I start first thing tomorrow morning."

That next morning, I packed a lunch for my little white dog and helped him put on his little white coat. I kissed him on top of his furry white head and watched him head off to work.

When he got to the end of our driveway, he turned and waved (which melted my heart), but I don't think he heard me when I whispered,

"Don't be gone long."

Before noon, Obie was back! I tried not to look too excited. "How was your first day as a scientist?"

"The lunch you packed was the best part of my day!" Obie replied. "But the lights were too bright and the walls were too white...making a morning nap practically impossible!"

"Sweet Obie, you don't have to be super-human," I reassured him. **"Here's a treat. Let me tuck you in for a nap. You must be exhausted!"**

The very next day, Obie walked into my sewing room and announced, "I have decided to become a handyman!"

"Oh!" I replied. I mean what else could I say?"

"Yes," explained Obie. "You see becoming a handyman will allow me to contribute to the Family Bottom Line."

"Family Bottom Line? **But you're my little white dog and I love you that way.**"

"Yes," said Obie, "But little white dogs can't help dad repair wooden fences, replace light bulbs, and trim back trees."

"Well, that's true I suppose, but I don't think..."

Obie raised a paw and interrupted my thoughts, "It's settled. I start my training program first thing tomorrow morning."

That next morning, I packed a lunch for my little white dog along with an extra snack and small brown leather tool belt. I kissed him on the top of his furry white head and watched him head off to Handyman University.

When he got to the end of our driveway, he turned and waved (which melted my heart), but I don't think he heard me when I whispered,

"Don't be gone long."

Before 10AM, Obie was back! I smiled warmly and said, "Did you learn a lot at Handyman University?"

"The lunch you packed was the best part of my day...and thanks mom for the extra snack, it was just the boost I needed as I walked to class." Obie sighed, "But they didn't have hammers my size and the nails were too sharp, making it virtually impossible for me to be productive."

Obie's head dropped a bit and his little shoulders slumped as he said, "I don't think I'll be of much help after all."

"Oh, sweet Obie, you don't have to be super-human,"
I reassured him. **"May I make a special treat for you and
can I sit with you for a while?"**

There were no grand announcements the next day or the day after that. But on the fifth day, Obie walked into the kitchen and made a grand announcement. "I have decided to become a chef!"

"Oh!" I replied. I mean what else could I say?

"Yes," explained Obie. "You see a chef is the perfect career choice for me."

"Career choice? **But you're my little white dog and I love you that way.**"

"Yes," said Obie, "But little white dogs can't help their moms in the kitchen. You're always making me food and working too hard!"

"Well, I don't think that's 100% true."

"No," replied Obie. "It's settled. I start culinary school first thing tomorrow morning."

That next morning, I packed a lunch for my little white dog along with an extra snack and a note that said, "I love you." I kissed him on top of his furry white head, adjusted his chef hat, and watched him head off to culinary school.

When he got to the end of our driveway, he turned and waved then blew me a kiss (which melted my heart), but I don't think he heard me when I whispered,

"Don't be gone long."

Obie took three steps, then turned back to face me. He stood in a bed of bright green grass and there was a radiant glow that burst through the tiny white hairs that covered his tiny white face. He was now 17 years old.

I knew he would forever be my baby.

We gazed at each other for a while, probably wondering what the other was thinking.

He broke the silence and said, "Mom? Can you just make me a treat instead and can I just sit on your lap for a while?"

"Oh, sweet Obie! Yes, Yes!" I replied.

**"You are my little white dog
and I love us this way."**

Special thank you to Dr. Corman at Loveland Animal Hospital
and her staff for taking such great care of our Westie friends.
We are fortunate to have our friends in your care.

Thank you also to the staff at MedVet of Cincinati, Ohio for
your loving care and expertise to keep our friends healthy and whole.

- The Baginski Family

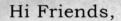

Hi Friends,

You're amazing just as God created you. We'll chat again in my next book.

Love you!
- Obie

To see Obie and watch this story on YouTube, visit PearlsInBloom.com/littlewhitedogvideo